AWESOME ANIMAL HEROES

JACK HANNA

LAUREN KUKLA

Consulting Editor, Diane Craig, M.A./Reading Specialist

Super Sandcastle

An Imprint of Abdo Publishing
abdopublishing.com

abdopublishing.com

Published by Abdo Publishing, a division of ABDO, PO Box 398166, Minneapolis, Minnesota 55439. Copyright © 2017 by Abdo Consulting Group, Inc. International copyrights reserved in all countries. No part of this book may be reproduced in any form without written permission from the publisher. Super SandCastle™ is a trademark and logo of Abdo Publishing.

Printed in the United States of America, North Mankato, Minnesota
102016
012017

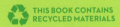

Editor: Paige Polinsky
Content Developer: Nancy Tuminelly
Cover and Interior Design and Production: Mighty Media, Inc.
Photo Credits: AP Images, Getty Images, Jack Hanna, Shutterstock

Publisher's Cataloging-in-Publication Data

Names: Kukla, Lauren, author.
Title: Jack Hanna / by Lauren Kukla.
Description: Minneapolis, MN : Abdo Publishing, 2017. | Series: Awesome animal heroes
Identifiers: LCCN 2016944660 | ISBN 9781680784350 (lib. bdg.) | ISBN 9781680797886 (ebook)
Subjects: LCSH: Hanna, Jack, 1947- --Juvenile literature. | Zoo keepers--United States--Biography--Juvenile literature. | Conservationists--United States--Biography--Juvenile literature. | Human-animal relationships--United States--Biography--Juvenile literature.
Classification: DDC 590.92 [B]--dc23
LC record available at http://lccn.loc.gov/2016944660

Super SandCastle™ books are created by a team of professional educators, reading specialists, and content developers around five essential components—phonemic awareness, phonics, vocabulary, text comprehension, and fluency—to assist young readers as they develop reading skills and strategies and increase their general knowledge. All books are written, reviewed, and leveled for guided reading, early reading intervention, and Accelerated Reader™ programs for use in shared, guided, and independent reading and writing activities to support a balanced approach to literacy instruction.

CONTENTS

Jungle Jack	4
Early Life	6
A Love of Animals	8
Hanna's Animals	10
Zoo Life	12
TV Star	14
Animal Adventures	16
Into the Wild	18
Working Hard	20
More About Hanna	22
Test Your Knowledge	23
Glossary	24

WHO IS HE?

JUNGLE JACK

Jack Hanna is an animal expert. He ran the Columbus Zoo in Ohio. He has also hosted TV shows. Hanna teaches people about animals and **conservation**. He is sometimes known as Jungle Jack!

Jack Hanna

JACK HANNA

BORN: January 2, 1947, Knoxville, Tennessee

MARRIED: Suzi Egli Hanna

CHILDREN: Kathaleen, Suzanne, Julie

WHO IS HE?

EARLY LIFE

Jack Hanna was born in 1947. His parents owned a farm near Knoxville, Tennessee. Young Jack loved farm life. The farm had many animals. Jack had pet dogs, donkeys, and rabbits. He rode horses with his brother and sister.

Hanna later brought his pet donkey to college with him! His name was Doc.

Jack (left) had a brother, Bush (middle), and a sister, Sue (right).

WHO IS HE?

A LOVE OF ANIMALS

Jack got his first job when he was 11. He began helping Dr. Warren Roberts. Roberts was the family's veterinarian. He was also the vet for a nearby zoo. Jack cleaned cages and fed animals. He dreamed of running his own zoo someday. In 1965, Hanna went to Muskingum College in Ohio. He met Suzi Egli there. They married in 1968 and had three daughters.

Hanna's favorite animal at the zoo was Ol' Diamond the elephant.

Hanna (back left) and Suzi (front right) with their daughters (left to right) Suzanne, Julie, and Kathaleen

WHO IS HE?

HANNA'S ANIMALS

Jack and Suzi moved to his family's farm. They opened a pet shop nearby. The shop sold cats and dogs. But Hanna also raised **exotic** animals, such as monkeys and young leopards. In 1972, one of Hanna's lions hurt a visitor. Hanna felt awful. He gave away his animals. He decided it was time to leave Knoxville and try something new.

The Hannas raised six lion cubs on their farm.

Hanna and Suzi also had parrots on their farm.

WHO IS HE?

ZOO LIFE

Hanna ran a small zoo in Florida. Five years later, he became the director of the Columbus Zoo in Ohio. Hanna improved the enclosures there. He made them more like the animals' natural **habitats**. Hanna taught visitors about the zoo's animals. He helped support **conservation** programs in other countries. The zoo became a success!

Hanna made a lot of changes to the Columbus Zoo. His first major change was placing the gorilla enclosure outside.

WHO IS HE?

TV STAR

Hanna began giving TV **interviews** about the zoo. In 1983, he appeared on the popular show *Good Morning America* (*GMA*). Hanna became a regular guest. And **audiences** loved him! Soon he was appearing on other TV shows. Hanna became famous.

Hanna showed the GMA viewers two baby gorillas. They were the first gorilla twins ever born at a North American zoo.

CONSERVATION WORK

ANIMAL ADVENTURES

Hanna loved teaching people about wildlife. Other zoos came to him for advice. So did **conservation** groups. In 1993, Hanna began his own TV show for kids. It was called *Jack Hanna's Animal Adventures*. Hanna taught his **audience** about animals and their **habitats**. The show ended in 2008.

Hanna filmed more than 150 episodes for Animal Adventures.

CONSERVATION WORK

INTO
THE WILD

In 2007, Hanna began hosting *Jack Hanna's Into the Wild*. This show also focuses on animals. It talks about different **conservation** groups. Hanna travels all over the world in the show. He visits cheetahs and elephants in Africa. He sees condors in South America. Hanna talks about problems such as **poaching** and **habitat** loss.

Hanna and Suzi at the 2011 Daytime Emmy Awards. Jack Hanna's Into the Wild *was nominated for Outstanding Children's Series.*

CONSERVATION WORK

WORKING HARD

Hanna still works to teach people about animals and their **habitats**. In 2014, he helped the Columbus Zoo open a new grassland exhibit. It features lions, zebras, giraffes, and more! Hanna also supports many **conservation** groups. He spreads his knowledge and love of animals all over the world!

The Columbus Zoo is one of the most popular zoos in the United States. It is home to more than 10,000 animals.

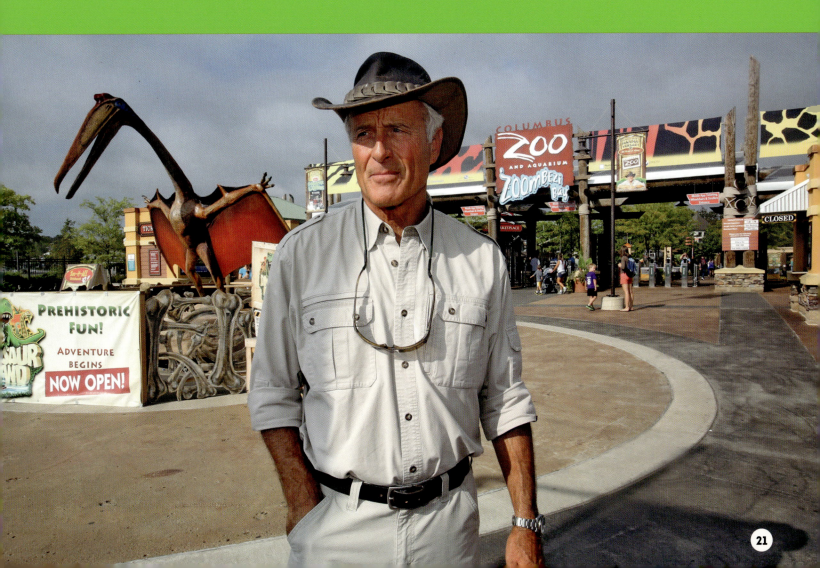

FUN FACTS

MORE ABOUT HANNA

Jack Hanna has 14 sets of SAFARI SUITS but only one hat!

As a child, Hanna had more than 100 PET RABBITS.

Hanna has written several BOOKS for kids.

Hanna has TRAVELED to every **continent** at least twice.

ABOVE AND BEYOND

TEST YOUR KNOWLEDGE

1. How old was Hanna when he began working for Dr. Roberts?

2. Hanna was the director of the Columbus Zoo.
   True or false?

3. What was the name of Hanna's first TV show?

THINK ABOUT IT!

What **exotic** animal would you most like to see? Why?

ANSWERS: 1. 11 2. True 3. *Jack Hanna's Animal Adventures*

GLOSSARY

audience – a group of people watching a performance.

conservation – the act or process of saving or protecting something.

continent – one of seven large land masses on Earth. The continents are Asia, Africa, Europe, North America, South America, Australia, and Antarctica.

exotic – very different or unusual.

habitat – the area or environment where a person or animal usually lives.

interview – a meeting at which someone is asked questions.

poach – to hunt or fish illegally.